MW00711232

This is a collection of poetry, prose, and fiction. Names, characters, places, incidents, ideas, or topics are either products of the author's imagination or are used fictitiously. Any resemblance to actual persons, living or dead, events, or moments is entirely coincidental

Copyright © 2020 Riley M Courtney

All Rights Reserved. No part of this book may be reproduced or used in any manner without written permission of the copyright owner except for the use of quotations in a book review.

First edition June 2020

Cover Design by Sloan Cochran
Book Design by Riley Courtney

Paperback ISBN : 978-1-0878-9230-6
Ebook ISBN: 978-1-0878-9231-3

ODE TO PERSEPHONE
A COLLECTION OF PROSE, POETRY AND STORIES

BY RILEY M COURTNEY

TO THOSE WHO INSPIRED THESE WORKS:
THANK YOU.

POETRY

Contents

Drown

Unfinished

The Boy and The Fly

In our Absence

Unfloral

Gaea

I lost My Voice

Mars

A Deadly Dance

Storm Speak

Cosmic Latte

Rat Boy

creamsicle Sneakers

Censor Yourself

The Impostor

Even Numbers

Water

The massacre of us

Beautiful

WHen I was

Futile Celebrations

Images of a Birthday

The Soul that Can

Glory and Romance

Monstro de Fuego

Death of a Matchstick

My Every Sign
Nude Beauty
Mountain Skin
Tree of Death
Quarantine
Unstable Dancer
Patron to the Follow
The Guilty Party Suffers
Sacred Possessions
Flightless Fish
Devotion
Stormy Morning
Us
With Age
Wet Flame
Pale Beauty
Rock Body
Dreamer's regret
All the bridges Falling Down
Love and War
Fateful Erosion
Stinging Cold
Me as Myself
Two sided war

DROWN

if I clung to you,
we'd both be dead.
Nothing but
four hands on a lifeboat
drowning behind a brick wall
frozen,
Looking left and right.

We are drawn to the sound of a light crunch;
soft in the dead of night.
Can One scream miles under salted water
or is there greater ease underground?

Could You imagine being six feet above ground
without the use of drugs?
and when You got there
would You have held my hand and pulled me up?
or would I have been your drug
for it is my shoulders You stand upon
in order to reach your six feet above.

Think of the Abyss we wished to venture towards,
Together.

Often I imagine
the way your fragile Glass vase of a body
would crumble if I could lay a Finger on you.
Had I dared to make that contact
it would be I to shatter,
despite your fragility.

Bring me down to rest
and let me invite You,
not with me but towards a Different Path:
a better one.
One I know you wouldn't choose for yourself
if given the chance.

Together we will walk to the ocean
taking divergent roads
and there,
in desperation
You shall shove me under to save Yourself.

Only,
as I go deeper,
 it will be I dragging your corpse
for I clung to You and
Now, we're both dead.

UNFINISHED

It's not yet complete;
Me, myself
and You.
Our final page has not yet surfaced.

Media killed Romance,
Not the other way around.
We expect love
with no heartbreak, until
The End.

Be your love anything but
Golden rays and monsoons,
you allow your blood to fill
with poison
and, in some cases,
You are the poison.

But us,
our flame is simply lost
Like a dancing candle
surrounded by wind.

THE BOY AND THE FLY

His adversary is his own domain:
an expansive plate,
covered in daunting Figures,
threatening to be altered
Even though he is the one doing the altering.

He begs the Figures he has locked himself with,
for coalition,
to form their own coven,
but he is quickly denied that freedom;
The figures have already begun
their own acts of exclusion,
of which he is no part of.

A broken bug,
unrestrained and blithe,
dances his way through a paranoid choreography
before plummeting towards the boy
as he consumes the remaining figures
resting against his plate,
alongside their dubious claims of community.

Between the two of them,
The Fly and The Boy,
their beliefs were proven to be
incompatible with one another

IN OUR ABSENCE

There's a constant notion of travel,
despite the inability.
Perhaps it's just the clouds,
singing woeful songs of companionship
in hopes that one day
their brass winged birds will fly again.

UNFLORAL

When I look at you,
I wish I could see flowers
for I find more beauty in them
thank Your Body could ever possess.

GAEA

She read like a patch of dirt.
She was boring;
masculine and linear.

So far,
she had been able to pass
as mortal,
but the shadows plague her damaged eyes
forcing her appearance to shift,
against her will.

Dirtied face,
seemingly hideous to those around her.
The voice inside her encourages
the idea that she is greater,
 otherworldly.
No more than a walking Goddess,
holding the planet
in her grievous palms.

I LOST MY VOICE

I lost my voice
screaming in my dreams last night.
Someone broke my bones
and stole my heart
but,
those pains were not the cause
of my yell.

I lost my voice
by walking into the
Cold
Empty
Room
and realizing the sting on my skin
was not my own.

I lost my voice
confessing my love to
the once tenderly caressed Teddy.
It had been carelessly handled by the air;
thrown out of my arms
and with that,
I lost my voice.

Mars has black eyes.
Deep
Black
Eyes.
She studies the sun
though in an identical sense
the sun studies her.
Without her knowledge,
of course.

Her shoulders extend farther than her hips,
but even they protrude past the welcome point.
In photographs
she hates it.

She refers to herself as
"The rectangle in the fruit bowl"
especially in comparison to her
Pear
and
Hourglass
figured friends.

In turn,
she prefers
the degrading element of providing them with
the unsolicited label of a delicacy.
They are not something to be eaten,
as delectable they may seem.
Nor are they a device on which we measure
Our Finite amount of time.

MARS

Mars,
However
is a rectangle in her own mind.

A DEADLY DANCE

bronze boned,
muscular build.
His body was sound
for he had been built by the Gods themselves.

Aside,
in a different arena,
adjacent categories,
laid his brother who goes by the name of Sister

She was underfed,
Underdeveloped;
A blade of grass
having allowed the wind to bend her into
a broken version of her identity.
She was but a scrawny stick
in a wood filled with oaks.

When the two met,
they were not to brawl
as one should expect,
nor to whimper,
but rather merge to an elegant song,
one with many variants
soon to be in its shadow.

Alongside their waltzing,
stood three large men
of the plump variety
ready to feast upon the First
Fallen dancer.
It was not the sister.

STORM SPEAK

Thunder growled,
like a prowling lion
in the distance.

Not rumbled,
Nor roared,
simply growled.

No light remained
aside from a single
Gas Flame,
held in the hands of a young boy
Tattered and worn
from the Unnecessary tending to his flame.

COSMIC LATE

The color of the universe
is painfully close to the color of
a much dreaded hallway.
The one struggled to tread by some
and forbidden to tread by many.

She is too similar to infection,
filing us through consecutively
as if we were
shots at a bar.

An upbringing in a poison filled world
would surely be treason.

RAT BOY

Gross boy, mimics a rat;
large yellow tail
long, not large.
When I said "no"
He ached.
We ached.

Rat boy:
shorter hair,
shorter nails,
broken teeth.
He looks rather silly
as he looks at me.

His smile too rugged,
too absent
and filled with anything
but regret.

CREAMSICLE SNEAKERS

Orange is such an aggressive color,
which is probably why I insisted on getting
Bright
Orange
Sneakers
for school in the 4th grade.

They were to make up for my
Passive
Virus
Ridden
Mind.

CENSOR YOURSELF

I am embarrassed
within my own walls
and about them too.

My mute button lingers,
so easily accessed,
and my fingers reach out for it
every time the notion of You
is brought forth.

I am going to speak today,
as I am surrounded by my own
Blood Coated Figures.

We are only separated by
three thick doors
and an expansive tunnel,
 yet you are always present in my mind.
making me fear the words
I used to sing.

Our space,
The one I had longed for since we met,
is the one place I feel this name is fit for.

Not even my bathroom,
with the light I use to study your every angle
is suit for naming you.

Not even in the bedroom
shall I call you what you are.

THE IMPOSTOR

I am an Impostor.
Feeling the sinful emotions
of the glutenous monkey
that resides within me.

He speaks not to those who ask,
and yet tells me his commands
I belong to him,
my Sinful Baboon.

Monkey.
Sing for me, do me a dance.
I am the voice to respond.
I am an impostor,
not your wishful puppet

Nothing more,
Nothing less.
My skin can come off
but I can guarantee
You will not like
what is underneath.

When I am uncomfortable
my voice resembles that of a crying cub;
almost startling to hear come out of
such a powerful creature.
I plea,
oh Monkey,
give me your aid.

Allow me,
your All Knowing Being,
to sing you a song with my cries.
Let me be your divine human:
Who ever said God isn't as mortal
as I?

Let me put on my show for you,
at the wishes of my captor
and in those moments,
worship me for
I am an impostor

EVEN NUMBERS

I am afraid of even numbers.
Above this line
is a line crossed out
hidden in spite of its power.

To speak a fear is to validate it
And there for,
I am afraid of even numbers

OFFERINGS TO COLOR RED

In a new day I dream
in the language of grass clippings and the scent of violets.
Taking the place of my nonsense images
hanging against my wall, lay their whispers
held up by nothing more than a weak strip;
mocking my strength.

Formed chemicals,
I'll them call *my* images,
swarm my thoughts.
In the new day,
they shall be fertilizer,
fueling the flames within me.
Make the grass grow faster
so by said new day,
we will have clippings to spare.

I'll leave them as offerings,
the Clippings and the Violets,
begging for more than them,
begging for the Color Red.
And when I fall short of their commands,
I'll ask them to spare me another day.

 When they return,
I leave them the grass clippings and violets
in abundance as compensation for my lacking.
In return,
They bring elegant tailed Bees,
to be powered by my chemical stained hands.
They bring a bucket of water
to cleanse the fertilizer that slipped into my eyes
trying to reach the grass in a too literal sense
despite my asking them not to.

It is not purification for which I ask,
and yet that shall be my destiny.

They will wash me by force
with the bees holding my arms,
tails at the ready,
all in the name of
Grass Clippings,
Violets,
and the Color Red.

WATER ME BEAUTIFUL

Take the shape of any and all containers,
expanding upon your bones
bringing yourself to a boil.

Every choice has air,
forming bubbles in your liquid body.
Only, you were not meant to flourish
as a liquid.

You hold the burden of all art on your shoulders;
haven forgotten how to create for yourself,
you remain
focused on a constructed,
versus all natural,
form of beauty.

Your skin does not flourish
with the rings of your age.
You are born a neutral,
and illiterate being,
who can tell the tales of the stars,
though struggle with the language of love.

Why study words
when they should be studying you,
Beautiful.

THE MASSACRE OF US

You are my false sense of satisfaction;
a celebration only you believe occurred.

We jump at the beginning
at the sound of a gun.
We dance,
but in solitude
in your burnt brick room of a house.

I could light you up,
despite your confident waltzing.
If I wanted to,
I could create a bonfire
out of the delicate skin of your corpse.
Yet, once dried,
leather is hard to pierce.
So, I spare you
where you couldn't spare me.

May we forever rest in Peace.

BEAUTIFUL

My shadow has scrawny legs
replicating those of a spider.

I am thin,
and my walk threatens
to pinch the skin from off your back
as if you were an apple
begging to be peeled.

My arms are replicates of my thin balance;
they both reach out towards the sky,
and drag against the floor in my stride.

My eyes are like the sun;
too bright to look at,
too big,
and yet, they find beauty
in the too small.

WHEN I WAS

I was so much more of a girl then:

My cargo shorts,
sequined shirts.
I felt royal

There was a boy,
we would play as children,
imuch different from now.
He craved adventure,
and with him, as did I,
though prior to him I'd sit out.

Funny what you'd change for a lover.
Even at age 9.

I was so much more of a monster then:

My essence was built by tears;
My way of begging
for attention.
Disgusting.
All my written words reflecting upon that evil.
But maybe,
it was the tears holding the malice intentions,
and my words were
simply their mirror.

I was so much more consistent then:

In our homeroom,
I found delicacy in the realm of their song,
before I found my own.
Every day,
My hair would catch on fire
and my scent kidnapped any life from my hands.
They told me it was beautiful,
my smell of burn,
and so I continued
until I too was a flame

I was so much more of a leader then:

Now,
I hesitate to ask
for help, for forgiveness, for a *name*.
Weariness has become my brand.
I am careful not to look up
out of fear my glance would lead to contact.

was so much more certain then:

Space was the goal,
not for me but for my ships.
I wanted to see the mountains
from atop the moon.
Less pride.
Death was certain.

No longer.

FUTILE CELEBRATIONS

Every time the sun goes down
Earthlings roam the streets.
"Freedom" they cry
Gathering,
Gloriously
Far from one another as they attempt to
Enjoy the life of those in solitude though
Drowning in the
Confining, yet spacious
City they have created.

IMAGES OF A BIRTHDAY

Unopened ribcage
out on display
in front of a child
excited, on his seventh birthday.

The record playing,
a gift from the dead man show,
was dragged against
roof shingles
emphasizing the wear of their words.

His father:
A body filled with metal
to the point where there is no more to spare..
His eyes are stapled shut
and in place of his teeth
lay rusted pennies.
There is no more milk,
how must he eat his cake?

Electricity fueled,
hullabaloo of a man,
The father stands motionless
next to the sobbing mother,
unaware of the robotics at play.

THE SOUL THAT CAN

was worth more than
the soul that Cannot.
For *obvious* reasons:

Optimism gains one half a glass of water.
People loved her, the soul
That Can.
She was broken from her journey,
regardless of the love she gained

To Can,
one first cannot.
To vote, women
Could not.
To live, the dead
Cannot.

The Soul that Can
is the lesson taught to children
through a train
for, perseverance is more realistic
in an object
than a human.

GLORY AND ROMANCE

are the equivalent to Gold and Red.
Though, not the ancient shade.
Rather the triumphant
and not one visible through kiss,
but rather decorating the skins of an apple.

Mercury is both a planet and a poison.
"You are a rusted silver"
I tell the shattered thermometer
who leaves its glass
to penetrate my feet.

Romance is both a planet and a poison,
but with you
it's neither.

MONSTRUO DEL FUEGO

I held him
until he bit.
His scent was,
shall I say,
Unruly
and his hair wreaked of mold.

Call it spontaneous,
our combustion,
but I was his flame
and he was my match;
our ignition was inevitable.

DEATH OF A MATCHSTICK

Ma,
I killed the flame

.

Then tell me, Son,
Why should the shadows still dance?
The dead to not sway
as the men before us.

Ma,
The flame lives on.

Then tell me, Daughter,
How is it we sit together in this room,
and I see you not?
Your voice is no echo of its passing,
but a warning of my own.

Ma,
I lit the flame.

Then tell me, Child,
Where shall the scent of smoke reside?
My lungs are not yet coated
and the match is not yet passed.

MY EVERY SIGN

The messy paintings
intentionally kept
under clothing:
bottom drawer.

The heavily decorated surroundings;
picture coated wall
flower soaked flag,
make the room a Home.

The cold,
though functional,
finger tips
often found, never lost,
pressed among paper and fire,
fueling creation.
Obsessively.

The photographs,
in a non physical state,
held an even closer and more private meaning
than the messy paintings.

The old blood stained sheets:
a sign of both maturity and its opposite.
The older they get
the less shall join them.

The lost afternoons
in a flooded basement
without a voice,
holding onto a wet match for life.

NUDE BEAUTY

To me,
nude beauty is the color green,
reflecting back at me
as I reflect on it.

I see myself as a tree
covered in too many vines,
arching from out of my middle,
for me to be anything but.

To the watcher in my mind,
and to only him:
the reflection apologizes in her own purified voice;
equally as vulnerable as my body.

He dances,
where I cry,
creating smaller, less prominent
reflections in my tears,
dropping to create a puddle underneath me.

The puddle turns into yet another reflection
emphasizing on something unknown to man:
Nude Beauty.

MOUNTAIN SKIN

Flat topped mountains
lay dormant;
previously exploded,
only there was no
Eruption.

Aside from the small,
bloodstained peak,
the mountain's skin remains unscathed;
separated by flesh like rivers
and thick dark jungles,
there was only one peak to the range.

T'was in rest;
rounded and unusual,
speckled white like the night sky
yet too similar to its clouds.

A flattened terrain
made travel easy,
though this was no sooth surface.
It lacked destination,
The Skin,
leading only to more
Flat Topped Mountains.
It was a journey well spent.

TREE OF DEATH

My identity gets distorted in the wind
as I lay upside down
against the noose like swing,
hanging from a melancholy tree.

My anger disturbs its peace,
the tree from which my death taunts.
It fills its roots with my passion;
My pain is its fertilizer.

It is not the tree of life,
but rather the tree of that happens to be living:
She composes herself in such a way
That simply cannot speak 'masculine,'
despite its attempts to,
forcing all of her branches into misshapen, but linear
and structural towers.

The tree of death be strong enough
to hold my swing,
and nothing more.

QUARANTINE

used to be such a horrific word.
Gone unspoken
even when alone
and left to confide with oneself.
Her implications
created the disgust in solitude.

She was a sickly white,
her entire body coated since her birth,
leaving her minimal room
or intentions
to grow.

She fills her latex shell
with an infectious blood
forcing her lovers to turn away.
She is not sick,
simply alone.

A mandated isolation;
left only with the company of a strangled bird,
suffocated by its own wings.
It too had been dipped in white paint.

UNSTABLE DANCER

When ballerinas spin
they pick a focal point on the wall
to keep them from getting dizzy.

My brain spins
only you sit in the audience,
surrounding me.

I cannot focus on my point,
though the spinning continues,
and the show must go on.

I'm stuck upside down
on the blue broken piece of metal
known as your heart.

I cannot be saved
from instant vertigo.

PATRON TO THE FOLLOW

A low Follow,
messiest of creatures,
guides me in her spite,
across the ends
and towards the middle.

Her back, the Follow's,
mimics the stars
forming a misguided halt in her confidence.

She wants me to be her captor,
but she is already mine
as I echo
following the unsettled trail she leaves for me
to be the Follow.

THE GUILTY PARTY SUFFERS

To be wrong
is not a sought invalidation
to the soul,
but rather an unintentional pain
begging to linger
in the deepest cavities
of our decent.

The ache often is suitable punishment
even when more should be required
and, it is
with heavy unfortunate.

SACRED POSSESSIONS

My skin is my own
begging for mercy,
having a conscience,
yet, falling to *My Will.*

Let me devour my skin tonight
under tattered sheets
between stained
and sacred walls.
let our intentions be visible to only us
and the Holy Spirit.

My blood is my own
coinciding with the moon.
I don't have control over her domain,
and yet
she holds full rein over mine.

I wish for it to spill
plaguing her oceans
and marking My Name on her intentions.

My skin is her predecessor
on which she spills herself
at my command.
I override the skin.

My eyes are my own
moving more like flies
than the steady stream
going down
My childhood memory's backyard.
My glance is not smooth,
it is as an unpaved road,
though it was once a marble
among bark.

FLIGHTLESS FISH

I'm in the woods;
a broken hearted green,
the same as another.

My window was broken,
shattered by a bird.
I am the window;
large crack like a splintering wood.
When we moved,
my mother begged for repair
of both me and the window

Ask me how I feel
when the birds are no more than fish
as we are no more than birds.

I aspire to be
everything I am not.
I cannot breathe underwater
nor can I fly or frolic or do any more than meditate.
But, tell me,
why am I surrounded by water from the sky
in the color green?

I am in the woods
but I belong in the house.
Where was I
when flames were our only smoke?
The way I respond to fire
is different in the way it speaks.

DEVOTION

Those who see the world
from a fragmented reality
shall be required to submit
to the Goddess
only they can see;
a frigid, yet judice figure above all.

Submit yourself,
she demands,
with only her malice intentions,
as she stands
positioned in the middle of her balcony.

She is the voice who encourages
The Impossible Soar;
a wingless flight towards a steadfast pool of gray.
It's liquid where they fall,
those who devote,
soon to be filled with their crimson waters,

The deep water fish
soaring around your room
as you attempt silence for *their* night
sing her song:
"You see me, now,
bring me your bones, later"

STORMY MORNING

Aggravated calm,
releasing energy through the roots
of which you sprout.

Forgotten tin of where we rest
within the fog covered windows,
finally finding peace from your world.

Rain Falls,
delicate and soft,
though it bites as much as it loves,
filled with the venom of a frozen snake,
dancing through a children's dream.

Snow falls
when dark meets light.
My old favorite shade would form
like curtains
closing in memories from today.

A filled camera rol
of supposed daydreams
ending in a broken record
and heartfelt screams.

Night falls,
mimicking rain
like an eye's mirror as it drops into the world,
filled with remorse
soon to be forgotten;
swept aside.

US

We'd spent so much Time
saying I love you
that we'd forgot about the Time
needed to question said love.

It was plentiful,
and neglected.

WITH AGE

I am too wrinkled
for companionship;
undeserving to have an excuse to avoid
The End.

Hell is cold,
and our arrival is inevitable.

WET FLAME

Like the sound of a drowning duck,
I breathe.
It's that simple,
yet I struggle,
allowing the water to create smoke
upon contact with my
Hot
Coal
Lungs.

I am not a smoker,
nor do I condone to similarities
and yet I am charred.

My body guzzles the air
as if I had spend my life in absence
and now, I lie awake
dry mouthed
and starving
like a flame with no air.

PALE BEAUTY

Today,
she dressed in gray,
covered in thy lord's name.

The word presents itself as a three dimensional image;
I turn her back and forth,
attempting to bring life to her lines.

She wears a halo,
one made of rose tinted gold
with its essence
coated in mud.

I wish I could call her beautiful
but against the moon,
she be not but vanished.
There is no beauty in the nose of a puppet,
protruding out and threatening
to enter any in its path.
Her beauty does not lie
like those of puppets;
She shall not be strung up.

She allows words,
Snake Tongued
Unrecognizable
Words,
to enter her vocabulary,
forming her every movement
into those of the puppets.
And it is I who holds her strings.

ROCK BODY

My body is the equivalent to a boulder:

I've been kissed before
every morning, every moment,
I've been kissed before.

Their beaks can eat away at me
as if I were their offspring.
They are my partner,
though I am their accomplice.

My enduring ache,
specifically not the word chronic,
is brought about by their mouths.
My brain is the equivalent to my stomach
in the sense that its only source is itself.

All my emotions reside in my neck
begging to be let out,
occupying their free time by scratching up the walls.

I prefer the birds to them.
They have no feathers to soften their bite,
and their greatest sin:
they cannot fly.

I am internalized;
sinking into my own
until I seek out
A singular burden
constantly echos my mind

As I sleep
all the rocks crumble
falling into the garden I like to call my bed
I am performing an avalanche to no one
I am my own audience
I am my own boulder

Dreamer's Regret

I want to breathe in more than I can;
Water.
Milk.
Song.
I want them to fill my lungs,
smother them with their nature.

I no longer want to think of my dreams
and smile.
Dreams are meant for frowns.
Dreamers are meant for the hopeless,
They find comfort in their optimism.

I want to dream in vivid colors
but when the wish becomes a reality
Strip me of such powers,
they are too much for me.

ALL THE BRIDGES
FALLING DOWN

I saw a bridge on my way here,
so intensely rusted over
and burnt.

There had been a fire
made of only the rain
and her warriors,
eating away at its stability.

I worry for the next train to pass.
In an intrusive fashion,
I allow my brain to cross it.
Stumbling across the burnt
broken
bridge
is not an easy feat.

The bridge and the beams
made of simple sticks,
nothing more than a child's art project,
It crumbled beneath me,
All hundred fifty four of me.

LOVE AND WAR

Is love still love
when disconnect is prevalent?
I question the sounds of my heart
when He is faced with absence.

My experiences with loss
are too unforgiving
for me to be familiar with the
concept of temperance.

You make me feel so unfinished,
so enlightened,
and yet I do not wish
to dance in the moonlight
with You;
Cleansing ourselves
and each other
from our suffering.

He is the hand
of which grips the sword
lodged within my skull
and yet you choose to comply.
You aid my fall
in your deliverance
to him.
Giving him his truest desire
is the equivalent of another sword upon my death

To shake his hand is to lose mine.
and in that sense,
I often allow you to corner me,
confining me to your darkest wits;
in his world
where there is no middle ground.

There is no neutral area in war,
you are either safe or in danger
and I
am in constant danger.

FATEFUL EROSION

My thoughts
try to assert themselves
into the minimal,
grayscale noise filling the space.

My mind is too focused
on the dusted sounds
that coat your bare body,
curing your pain.

I imagine the sand,
now creeping towards your eyes,
Blinding you,
leaving me gracious in your absence.
I allow the sand to determine my values,
as it scratches through my body
trying to get to you.

STINGING COLD

Only my hands and my ankles are cold
in an advertently sexual way.
They are too vulnerable
to the way they refuse to
melt into their shields
as the other parts are hiding.

They continue to take the bullets
refusing to
"play dead"
and yet, I beg,
for I feel the pain
they refuse to acknowledge

ME AS MYSELF

I wonder how others see me:
Am I wet,
like my voice,
nothing more than
a swelling ocean of anger?
Am I shrill
or does my voice grumble
as it does in my head?

I dread the days
I appear on film
sounding so robotic,
too condensed.
as if I consumed
the wings on which he fled.
I am only hungry
for what you bring to me,
and he is too far to be brought.

and he is too far to be brought.
the passion in my body.
I've been too bent
So I suppose you find me moldable.

TWO SIDED WAR

Walls grow
where flowers were expected to.
Big
and Small
reside on opposite sides,
suffocating in their separation.

The walls are beautiful,
almost as flowers would be
but grey doesn't equate to passion.

Flowers are delicate,
capable of trampling
by the big, as the small.

In response, we are the median.

TELL ME I AM SAFE

even when my
voice
arms
legs
mind
have been taken from me,
Tell me I am safe.

TENSE HOLD

My being is stretched
as if I were a water balloon
only, I am allergic to water balloons.
My skin burns my skin.

I am screaming
in this constant torture:
Be aware,
be aware.
Hear me and my signals
preparing to go to war
with my body.

PROSE

CONTENTS

PERFECTLY PASTEL

TO LOVE A GODDESS

OF TALL GRASSES

LETTERS TO PERSEPHONE

END OF WOMAN

MONSTER IN MY HEAD

ODE TO APHRODITE

MY EDEN

LIFE IN THE CIRCUS

I once found beauty in simplicity. Two colored, one word, barely an image in its name. I found comfort in pastels and the calm they made me feel, so much so that I made an effort to become those pastel colors.

My body cleansed itself of any dark it held and in its emptiness, began to fill me with light pink. My infatuation with this color grew and grew to the point where it became my only personality trait.

I was light pink.

When she, the baby pink my bones now consumed, lost her umph and became out of trend, she died. All the other colors had fled my body and broken my bones leaving me with an empty shell and the corpse of the once beloved color. I had become so dark, I was light.

It created such submergent pain, I no longer knew how to process anything but this seemingly chronic issue.

My spirit longed for the light colors so much that in its desperation, it reached for anything it could find. Those I found became more permanent residents who took hold of both my head and heart along with everything else in between. They were dark, and I was not used to their morals.

I felt greedy being in possession of so many colors and patterns, not a single one of which matched with the other, but in my greed I felt a new found beauty and love, and passion for both myself and my body.

The beauty found in simplicity had transformed itself into a love found in painful colors and passionate clashings.

PERFECTLY PASTEL

To Love a Goddess

To the intruder with the round cheeks and chin, soft looking hair but not in the sense that it would feel soft. Rather it, in essence is a cloud.

To the poet with the medium wash jeans, an almost bright shade of blue, not quite reaching your ankles but almost grazed the tops of your short ankle-length boots with a perfectly length heel for you.

To the Goddess men would like to recognize for they have fallen for you lifetimes before. Who wouldn't.

To the Lonely Little Bird whose wings were once made of a towering darkness, but have now returned to nothing but a charred twig. There is beauty even in you.

To the Goddess whose voice was just as soft, if not more so than her hair. I watched as you danced around the room while you told us the birth of your wonders. The world has found themselves at your command, forever in love with your essence.

I will never allow you, My Child, to walk in the naked grass regardless of its calming intentions. You shall be broken from the feet up, given pins and needles through your precious toes by a soft blow.

Rather, I will encourage you, My Child, to fear not the sting but rather find discomfort in the strands as they slither between your base and up into you, My Child.

How could we blame the bees for their stings when the face of your pain is the ever penetrating blades now engulfing you whole, My Child.

OF TALL GRASSES

LETTERS TO PERSEPHONE

Aside from the light created by the tiny gas powered flame, there was only the occasional lightning strike to create shadows of every solid object in this room. To be alone at such change would be terrifying, not yet understanding that nothing waits for him in the shadows.

Persephone awaits his word, making it increasingly more important that he got the letter out by morning, despite his fears in the dark. The rain had taken the skin from off his body and he found his bones close to shattering. His fingers were frozen solid and he longed for the sun to turn the nights worth of rain into a thick, hot fog, made to swallow his now stable body against the floor.

Perhaps, when he finished her letter, he would find some warmer clothes. If he finished her letter.

At my end, I wish to have only women around to make up for the places no women were allowed. We would fill the ocean with our bodies. Our breasts would range in size, alongside hips, legs, height; we are each our own difference.

It would be so different from a funeral. We would walk the streets, my corpse in the middle, and their souls surrounding me in the place my casket should be. It would be so different from a march, for there is no protest, no purpose other than to walk.

And walk we do, only the dead cannot walk so I simply rest as if a queen among my servants. We are equals despite my body residing upon their shoulders, for I shall do the same for them upon their deaths.

END OF WOMAN

MONSTER IN MY HEAD

I no longer fear the monster *under* my bed for the two have become one and the same:

My monster and my Bed. At night I am surrounded by its white slits as eyes, emitting enough light to just barely keep me thinking while I should be asleep. I rest, moments away from its mouth filled with a dark and cold air despite the warmth of the room I reside in.

Though the fear is still relevant, there are days I greet my monster, who has become my bed, with my rose thorn stained cheeks and glistening eyes, ready to shake its hands and become a part of whatever horrors live inside it. In our dealings I expect the monster to help me, and though it never does, I continue to return to it day and day again.

Most summer nights I would ask his eyes to change color. I'd ask for them to become a burnt red, a broken red. If not asking too much of him, I'd ask to be turned to liquid, almost like blood but with more meaning.

In respect and content with my pain and discomforts, the monster obliged and did as I asked, knowing this small favor would turn into a lifestyle for me.

I was reliant on *My* Monster.

The longer I slept with him, the more I began to become him. Soon, my arms were engulfed in his liquid red-white slits of eyes and covered with a thick layer of fabric, suffocating in the heat of the room.

I resided in his stomach when I slept: both frigid and shallow, I, much like my bed had become my monster.

My appetite grew as I remained inside him. The colder I became, the more I lost and the deeper I fell into his being.

I craved substance and begged to devour his cold frozen emptiness, and soon found that the monster still remained but he was me rather than me being him.

My eyes remained intact and though there were days he would escape my abyss, mine being much smaller than his, he remained in my prison.

I no longer fear the monster inside of me.

Bring your word into my room, Aphrodite, and use my eyes to view your items as they produce a child strong enough to conquer with nothing more than the word love. Dress him in silk night wear and tell him to look outside for my haunting soul. If I follow your orders, Aphrodite, it will be my naked tombstone in the ground, and it will be before I am to finish your offerings.

The pink light you use to fill my room must be from your body, for I stare at your figure from my bed as my resilient mind begs you for slumber. You emphasize my needs, Aphrodite.

Feel my orchids as they flutter across my desk to the sweet song of death. But, feel them not with a handshake as to not destroy their beauty, rather feel them with your mind, Aphrodite.

Join me in my own fearful slumber and envision them burning, my own eyes alongside love itself. I ask you to leave me my heart, of all things, for I only require it and the cavity you left within it to fuel my dreams.

ODE TO APHRODITE

My Eden

Smoke rolls across the floor making it impossible to see my feet. Despite being less than an object, it seemed to sing. To him, the voice sounded heavenly and spoke in tongues he didn't think he could understand, and yet he did.

To her, it rang and lingered like nails on a chalkboard. The voices spoke in no tongue to her, but simply harmonious notes seared together.

The sky was unlike one known to present man for it was a peached shade of orange, creating a soft glow against the world where there would have been a cool, harsh light.

It was a broken world, begging for my wrongdoings, and yet it was only my pleaing voice she heard. I was the snake, crawling among the smoke. I offered apples as means of hospitality, and she accepted. What guest wouldn't? I was not the curse of humanity, but rather they were the curse of me. Sin is not a fearful thing. Neither are snakes.

Often, she felt like she lived in the circus.

The walls of her own little clown house were ever so bright, so much so that they kept her from sleep upon multiple occasions. At once, it was her dream, child-like and comfortable. With white liner, soon to represent much more to her than something to separate the colors, between each and every board.

Any color one could imagine being on the walls was the vein in a sense. While the palate was strictly pastel, she saw a deep red hidden between the baby blue and millennial pink shades. One wall, the supposed 'accent wall' was covered in only the yellow, to which she soon grew bored and began to coat that wall in butterfly stickers.

LIFE IN THE CIRCUS

STORIES

CONTENTS

MOONLIGHT DEATH
BUY ME THE STARS
GOOD GIRL GONE HAPPY
WELCOME TO HELL
ESCAPING MY OWN
DISCUSSIONS OF LIFE
CHOICES

MOONLIGHT DEATH

The overwhelming light blue haze streams through my window after I made the fatal decision to leave it open. After hours of trying, I had concluded that tonight would be a sleepless one.

Giving up, I grabbed my phone from under my pillow and saw at least a hundred texts from unknown numbers. It was 1:17 in the morning and while unknown calls weren't uncommon during the day, but this was well past their typical hours.

They all read the same message, though some seemed to be in a different language. I assumed those said the same thing. Two messages were from my friends but even they were verbatim:

The moon looks beautiful tonight. Take a look.

Under all the texts was an emergency message:

Do not look at the moon, whatever you do…

The text continued but my attention was directed elsewhere. I become fixated on the light projected onto my wall from the window, fearing whatever it is that lies above me.

The message from the government probably held all the answers to what was roaming through my head but amidst my sleep deprivation, combined with whatever minimal effect the light was having over me I disregarded any want to check the message. My eyes remained fixated on the light blue rectangles painted on my walls.

The air was cold against my skin, as if begging me to not get out of bed. But I did against its wishes. I wish, looking back, that I had found more comfort in the air than I did. Nothing, from the moment my eyes met the moon's, would ever even whisper comfort again.

I am alone. No more moonlight, please.

BUY ME THE STARS

When I was younger, I would overhear father talking on the phone a lot. At first, before he knew I was listening, most would be in English up till I started questioning. Then, he switched to something I couldn't describe if I tried.

Mom said he wanted to buy the stars and their planets for me and hang them in my room for when I can't sleep. She told me he wanted to cure my fears, and fill the darkness with their essence.

She told me they'd light everything just enough for me to see the chair at the end of my bed wasn't anything more than that. They would turn the 8 limbed monster in my closet into nothing more than a couple hanging coats. The shadow hanging over my desk was not from a peeping stranger, but simply the shelf from above. The pile on the floor was not a corpse, waiting to become undead and eat me alive in my sleep. It was simply my dirty clothing from the day before.

The thought of the universe being in my room was comforting, but I still couldn't figure out where it was my dad could possibly get the stars and their planets for my room.

And I didn't believe he would.

Until he did.

GOOD GIRL GONE HAPPY

Her entire high school experience would be summarized into a single sentence: She longed to join a band, but didn't. Every experience, or rather lack thereof, was burdened by the idea of "trouble" without the concept that trouble = temporary. The week before, the majority of her hair fell victim to a pair of scissors and a bottle of bleach for which she was already facing the consequences for, this would not add much to her punishment.

With her she had only the light pink guitar gifted to her as a child, which she poorly learned how to play only a couple hours before.

Her bike remained in the shed but it was the most accessible thing in there, and according to her maps it would only be an 8 minute ride given her guitar wouldn't complicate matters too significantly. With one foot out the door, she begins to question what she's about to do. She belongs with him, there's no question in that.

Her only hesitancy comes with the fear in what she's about to do. He hasn't seen her new hair yet, and he can only imagine his reaction being negative. She's only been playing for a couple hours, and now she's about to go play in front of an entire room full of people, and for the first time in her life, the thought of that excited her.

Once she jumped from the not too high bedroom window, all thoughts of going back had left her. There was no question of regretting her decision, but she was certain she would regret not going.

By the time she reached the party, the parking lot had already been half filled with cars, so she pulled her bike over into one of the neighbors bushes, and hid it there. She didn't even care if it did manage to get stolen. Her entire night was completely carefree. As it should be after being cooped up for the first 18 years of her life.

Instinctively after removing her helmet from atop her head, she threw it into the bushes and attempted to run her hands through her hair, only to be met with the tiniest of hairs she had left upon her head. She smiled this time at her boyfriend's reaction, knowing her fear was only temporary in her escape. He was going to love it, she was certain.

Throwing her guitar over her shoulder, she began to strut into the party, leaning back with every step she took. A couple people gave her weird glances, but no one paid her any more attention than they had before.

She went into the house through the back door, just as Jaxson had told her to do. It wasn't a formal invite to the party, and she didn't even know the person whose house it was but when she walked in it felt right. She knew this was where she was supposed to be.

Jaxson turned towards her at the sound of the garage open, and his mouth instantly dropped, though his lips remained curled upwards hinting at his satisfaction with her haircut.

"I didn't think you'd actually do it," he says in disbelief.

"Come to the party or shave my head?" he sets down his own guitar before making his way over to her to give her a hug.

"Both, honestly." She smiles, content with challenging both her and his expectations for herself.

"You look amazing," he runs his hand over her almost smooth head, and then pulls her guitar from over her head for her. "Now, are you ready for your first ever band rehearsal?"

Her face was bright as she followed Jaxson. All of the band looked equally satisfied with her appearance. In this moment, she was at peace in the place she had thought she'd be most uncomfortable, and she loved it.

WELCOME TO HELL

As he was walking towards the house,a top hat materialized on his head and he suddenly felt very nauseous. He removed the hat to reveal a pile of new found treasure spilling out across his head, though he put no thought towards that as he continued to ralf up the thirteen shrimp, six packs of swallowed gum, and a whole bottle of vodka.

He made his way, sloppily and stumbling between every step he took, to the other side of his car, receiving many odd looks from couples making love in the passenger seat of their cars.

Someone attempting to leave nearly runs him over before he finally makes his way to his destination, his car.

"Some one had a rough night," He scans the area, puke filled top hat still in hand, not having processed its appearance, but sees no one.

"You're telling me," he whispers back, not expecting anyone to hear him and being under the impression that the voice was nothing more than his head. He couldn't have possibly known it was so much more.

A high pitched screaming began to ring throughout his head, causing his legs to buckle and mind to shatter as if he was a glass and the voice was a hammer.

He cries out, "Help," right as the speaker reveals herself. He draws the attention of only her with his cries, though with his eyes squeezed shut he doesn't notice her. Her mouth is open as if she were the one screaming, but the sound only echoes around his head.

She has dirty blonde hair, holding an impressive amount of shine as it dances around in the moonlight. In the dark, it appears to be a simple light brown. Her eyes were covered in an ashy, smudged black eyeliner as if she had been crying. The mess in her style seemed too intentional for it not to be beautiful.

Then the second he opened his eyes, her mouth closed and the screeching throughout his head halts. No one around them from the party looks up, or even hears his pain. Almost immediately his eyes dilate an abnormal amount even for the night.

She was the owner of his top hat, and smiled to see it filled with his vomit.

"Welcome back, Lucifer" she spoke, smirking towards him in an almost daunting fashion. He was happy to see her, though embarrassed that he was summoned while partaking in such mortal extravagances.

"God, I will never get used to that. Nice to see you, Sasha," he grimaces towards her in a polite, yet demeaning tone. "Don't you have better things to be doing?" he snarls towards her, in reference to her simply standing and watching him in a mocking tone. She smiles back at him, and starches the hat from his hand and widening her eyes at him in attempts to be seductive. Her eyes were dilated similar to his, only they had a red gloss hanging over them.

She curtsies towards him, in an uncomfortable mannar per usual, and melts into the river alongside her family.

Despite the fiery hot feeling in the air when met with the river, there was no humidity and Hell was rather dry. His skin began to dry as any moisture he had went into the air transforming him into a red scaly figure.

It wasn't a comfortable transformation. Nothing about Hell was comfortable.

ESCAPING MY OWN

All of my family, friends, everyone I know surrounds me. They just stand there and watch me. There isn't much for them to do, but there is so much I want them to do. I want them to save me, I need them to save me. Water streams from the corners of my eyes burning my face, making more and more liquid come out. I have never experienced anything like it in my life. Everything is so new.

I'll never see them again. Meaningless words fall from the tip of their tongues to try and calm me down. They say it's okay, that I'll live. They tell me that everything will work out in the end, they say they'll miss me.

They won't miss me, there isn't anything to miss. I never knew any of them, not even my own mother. I lived in a house for 15 years with them, ate the food they gave me and trusted them. I'll miss them, still. They all were a huge part of my life, and even the fact that knowing that they wouldn't be part of it anymore is enough to break me.

I'm going to die. There is no escaping it. I knew I was going to die for weeks now. My stomach starts to flip around, and my head starts to go haywire. The tears oozing down my cheeks start to get heavier. My mind automatically drowns everything out. The guards come in from the opposite side to get me. My family just stands there, watching me go. No waving. No hugs. They just stand there.

My emotions bubble up inside of me. I turn down a few halls, then find a huge tube standing in front of me. Guards are everywhere, slowly pressuring me into the tube. The burning anger of so many years starts to rise to the surface. Everything starts pouring out of me at once. I'm already going to die, why not give them a better reason to kill me?

I felt my stomach drop before I felt the floor fall. It felt like flying but I knew it wasn't. The floor just gave out, dropping from right beneath my feet. This isn't right. This shouldn't be happening. I didn't do anything wrong. No one could save me now, not even gravity itself.

The cool darkness surrounds my bare arms. Everything around me is so plain, so simple. It's like staring at a black wall.

What happens now?

I'm still falling, I think but there's no way to be sure. The fluttering sensation twirling around in my stomach is still present, but who's to say that isn't part of death?

I can still picture the way the words rolled off of the tip of my tongue, and how everything around me seemed to stop when I did it. I can almost hear my own voice ringing in the darkness around me. It was a simple mistake, I had seen it happen so many times. Anyone could have made it.

My feet hit something hard. I feel my legs give out when I try to stand on it. Small, but bright lights start to appear all around me, almost as if they were in a pattern. The stinging on my face cools down, but my emotions don't.

Is this what it's like? Is this how I die? This can't be it. There is supposed to be people and light. It's supposed to be bright.

I'm supposed to go to heaven.

I sit down on the ground, and bring my legs up to my chest as I watch the lights dance towards me in unison. I let my palms get drenched in sticky sweat and my mind get lost in my thoughts.

I have nowhere to go, nothing to do, no one to help me. I don't even know if I'm dead. That's an easy fix though. I could make that happen in a second if I wanted to. I have too much power over my own life. Too much control. Too many things that could go wrong. And it would all be my fault.

There is no way to make myself stop thinking. There is no way to go back to my normal life. Even if I could, everything would be ruined anyway. My friends are gone, not that I ever had any. My family won't remember me and no one will even know what I look like. I could do it. I could end it all right now. Maybe already have. My thoughts would stop and my mind would be at peace, but the lights keep me from it, slowly approaching and promising some ounce of meaning.

There has always been that one dream; A dream full of my insecurities. Everything that I ever did to get me to where I was now. How many memories went into this moment? How many things had to happen for me to be here now acting like this?

The lights halt, having been in the same place for so long. They mimic the slight good that lives in the shadows of my heart, and I can't help but wonder if that is where I am now. They punished me with my own mind.

And I deserve it.

DISCUSSION OF LIFE

The sounds of their muffled voices when amplified by the cave walls was heard by what seemed like a nation of people. Their shadows which would seem like nothing but a blur in such fire light paired with their voices and there was no doubt about their figures.

They were cold and rough. Their touch could have frozen the oceans with ease. They were the warmth of a thousand stars. They were the rise and the fall. They were the rain and the leaves. They were the only thing stable about change.

Some spoke of new life, dreaming of the ground and its recovery from the harsh winter. But when put in a room as they were now, in the dark, one couldn't see these differences, one could only hear their voices.

The Cold's voice was by far the loudest as it echoed farther than any of the others. His opinion seemed so definitive when compared to theirs. He spoke of the fate of this child, this unborn child, so effortlessly. He spoke of the child's end with no regards to any possible in between. The thought of it puts him at ease. Death was his coping mechanism.

Others spoke of the rest of the child's life, not caring if the Cold and his allies listened. Together they formed the year, but when apart, they were nothing but a few measly weeks.

Those prone to life spoke, telling Cold the boy would be the needed change to the world. They spoke of it being for their benefits, but those who rose and fell questioned it, following in the Cold's grumbles. They thought any footprints this child would make would be with the dead, they said the words that made even the Cold tremble.

They all spoke of his eyes, for the unborn eyes of the child were almost as important to their story as the story itself. All of them together would agree upon one thing: His eyes. His eyes held all of their voices and all of their shadows, they held the bickering of the Cold, the Sun, the Life and the Fallen.

"He's to be the end." The harshness in his voice shook not only the room but those in it as well. "He's not this glue you all speak of, he's not what's supposed to build us back away from this fire that's soon to be. He's to be the new spark ready to set us all ablaze." The others stared at him in dismay, frustrated with Cold's harsh tone. He was never easy to persuade.

"But we must recover. If it's not to be him, then who will it be?" She snaps back at him, with such smoothness in her voice.

"We can recover without a so-called hero." He paused, not having spoken yet in this gathering. "The people, our people, they find such a beauty in the dead, they could enjoy this. Everything must fall."

"But if it falls, there's still hope they need to have peace of mind it will rise. They rely on this hope to get them through the wind."

"No, we mustn't focus on the parts leading to it, we mustn't worry about our people. They're made for adaptation, we should know. Focus on his eyes," the Cold barks at the others "Focus on the way they will seem not how they seem."

His comment leads to the bickering of others, making it unclear to tell who's speaking. The points they made never fit in with their past points, but they seemed to stay on topic. There was a sense of worry in all of their voices, not in the moment type of fear though, the fear for the future. This all went on for what seemed like hours, until the cold spoke again.

"Enough, the child is to come within the hour and we have yet to make our decision. We are not God, but in this case and this case only we must play him." He paused as if waiting for a reply but when he didn't get one he continued. "We have more control over this child's life than we do our own, and if we think this child is to shape the world as much as we think he will then we must choose how to use this power and chose it wisely. This isn't the child's fate to be worrying about, and I reckon I am contradicting every past word I've spoken, but this is the fate of more to rest on our shoulders."

"New life." she mutters under her breath. No one could see her eyes in such little light, but they felt her panic. "New life." The murmurs spread around like a wildfire among the voices. They spoke in present fear now as the first new life to speak climbed upon the table, they all sat around and muttered the few words the people all feared. The Cold watched the child's eyes be brought to life before him.

"The child's cries are among us now. New Life is now among us."

CHOICES

His name was Avery. He wore a long bright yellow jacket that would typically drag behind him on the ground but due to the impressive amount of layers underneath it, his sides and shoulders puffed out just enough to keep it from the sludge covered sidewalks. In the crowd full of black, grey and blue shirt-length coats, he stood out.

No one paid him any attention nonetheless, for the coat was almost always a part of his attire. Only his layers were seasonal.

He stood in the front of the lunch line on this specific Tuesday afternoon, hesitating to make a choice between the three options they had available. He was too busy contemplating how this singular decision would influence his well being in the future. Each choice he made was detrimental to the next, and the uncertainty was enough to kill him. At least, if the choice didn't get to him first.

Those behind him stood impatiently for about 12 minutes before they decided to just go around him, creating minor chaos throughout the room but nothing the lunch ladies weren't used to.

Another 7 minutes passed before it was just him and them, the lunch ladies. Per usual, their every day exchange began:

"What are you thinking today, kid?" The woman behind the counter asked. She was large, Avery liked her for that reason. He thought she looked like him with his layers on. Her question frustrated him though causing him to sigh and storm out, just as the bell rang. Maybe tomorrow he will eat.

"Hey Avery." Jake stands outside the lunch room on his phone, suddenly becoming more alert as Avery walks past him. "No lunch again?"

Routine.

"They wanted me to choose. When will they learn," he exclaims as much as he can in his monotonous, somewhat dull voice, just as he does every day. "When will they learn, choice means death." He looks straight ahead, starting to lose speed and his breath and finds sudden discomfort in his layers.

"Could you explain this all to me one more time please?" Jake asks, not recognizing Avery's signals of desperation.

"No."

Silence.

"Why not?" Again, oblivious to the signs.

Avery began to hyperventilate. He was too hot, too many layers too big a coat. It was suffocating.

His comfort item in this moment was the one thing bringing him the most discomfort.

ACKNOWLEDGMENTS

There are many people to thank when it comes to the creation of this collection. Going through the entire process was long, and took the efforts of so many people. Starting with the writing of the first draft. This entire collection came from one notebook written during my sophomore year of high school, so I would like to thank my teachers for allowing me to write in class, even when I should have been doing something completely different.

Two of the biggest aids during this process were my best friends, Annabel Howe and Mia Leyland, who both helped edit and polish up the collection. Without them, it would not have been nearly as pretty as it is now. Similarly, I'd like to thank my cover design artist, Sloan Cochran. She created the face of Ode to Persephone, and it could not look any more perfect.

The 'production team' is fairly small, but there are many other people who had a signifigant inflence on me and Ode to Persephone. My entire family was extremely supportive from the start, as were all my friends and other relatives. I'd also like to thank all of my supporters and friends from Instagram for providing me with the much needed support to create this. Thank you.

CPSIA information can be obtained
at www.ICGtesting.com
Printed in the USA
LVHW092343180421
684865LV00006B/395

9 781087 892559